It's happening again...

Lucy looked down to find that her uniform was splattered with blood. Hesitantly she touched her hand to her face and felt something warm. And wet. She drew her hand down – it was covered with blood as well.

It's just a nose bleed, Lucy told herself.

She was wrong. Her eyes fluttered shut, her knees buckled and she fell to the floor, shaking. Strangers gathered around, staring down at her.

Lucy began to speak in slurred, trance-like words: "Nobody's gonna spoil us nobody's gonna spoil us nobody's gonna spoil us nobody's gonna spoil us nobody's gonna. . ."

D1354030

Other X-Files books in this series

Voyager

THE X FILES"

Empathy

Novelization by Ellen Steiber

Based on the television series
The X-Files created by
Chris Carter

Based on the teleplay
written by Charles Grant Craig

HarperCollins*Publishers*

To Clinton Van Zandt, a former
supervisor with the FBI's
Behavioral Science Unit,
with gratitude for his patience.

Thanks also to Thomas Harlan, Sr.,
and Michael Korolenko for the woods
of the Pacific Northwest.

Voyager
An Imprint of HarperCollins*Publishers*
77–85 Fulham Palace Road,
Hammersmith, London W6 8JB

This paperback edition 1997
    2   3   4   5   6   7   8   9

First published in the USA by HarperTrophy
A division of HarperCollins*Publishers* 1997

The X-Files™ © Twentieth Century Fox Film Corporation 1997
All rights reserved

ISBN 0 00 648328 3

Set in Goudy

Printed and bound in Great Britain by
Caledonian International Book Manufacturing Ltd, Glasgow

Chapter One

Jim Larken, the photographer who was taking the freshman-class pictures for Valley Woods High School, didn't pay much attention to the girl with long, honey-blond hair who stepped in front of his camera. He'd already taken more than fifty photographs and would take another two hundred before the morning was out. As far as Larken was concerned, all high school kids looked the same. "Name, please?" he asked.

"Amy Jacobs," the girl answered as she centered herself in front of the camera. She was wearing an off-white button-down blouse and a short plaid kilt-style skirt.

"Okay, now show me those pearly whites," Larken said. A sweet, unself-conscious smile appeared on Amy's face. Larken's flashbulb strobed, blinding her for a split second. Then he wrote her name on his list, next to a number. "Okay, Amy," he said. "Fill out your address card. Next in line, step up."

Amy crossed the gym to a long table where other kids were filling out address forms.

"Hey, Ms. Fashion Model." Amy looked up to see Bobby Snyder, one of the cutest guys in her class. He offered her a pen. "So how does it feel to be immortalized for the yearbook?"

Amy glanced at him curiously. She was never sure if Bobby Snyder actually liked her or just liked teasing her. "Oh, it was incredible," she said in a deliberately dry tone. "I'm sure it will change my whole life."

"It just might," he said, grinning at her.

"Next!" the photographer called.

A thin, gawky boy stepped in front of the blue screen and Larken peered through his lens. There was another strobe flash, and the photographer nodded at the kid, then rewound and removed the film from the back of the camera.

"Name, please?" Larken asked.

"Dennis Mallard," the kid answered.

"Okay, Dennis," the photographer said. "Fill out the address card." He turned to his assistant. "I need a reload, Carl."

Carl Wade, Larken's assistant, was sitting on one of the big metal cases they used to carry the lights and tripods. Wade was a middle-aged man with a thickening waistline and wavy blond hair streaked with gray. He was gazing off across the gym, his pale blue eyes resting on a pretty girl in a plaid kilt.

"Carl," Larken repeated, more impatiently this time. "Hey—I need film."

Wade finally looked up at his boss. "I haven't loaded it yet," he said.

"Why do you even bother coming in if you're not going to do your job?" the photographer demanded. Annoyed, he got up and reached for a film canister himself.

Wade stood looking at him helplessly for a moment. Then, when he was sure no one was watching him, he let his gaze return to Amy Jacobs.

Amy was talking with a good-looking boy as she filled out the address card. The boy didn't matter. But the girl did. She had that look—childhood innocence tinged with the first bloom of heartbreaking adult beauty. Wade couldn't take his eyes off her. There was something much more than simple admiration in his gaze. Something much darker . . .

A pale hand pulled on a metal chain, and a single red light bulb popped on. The hand belonged to Carl Wade. He was standing in a dark, windowless basement that he'd converted into a makeshift darkroom. He needed only a few things: a sink, an easel, the enlarger he'd bought years ago secondhand, and the scarred wooden table where he was now working.

He picked up an X-Acto knife, slid in the small razor-sharp blade and screwed it tightly in place. Then he lowered it to the table and began to slice into an object that should not have been there: a 5 x 7 photograph of Amy

Jacobs, a photograph taken that day at the school. She was so pretty. So young. He reached out a finger and stroked her hair.

Using the knife, he traced the outline of Amy's body with great delicacy. His mouth hung open as he worked. He discarded the background of the photo, then set her image on the table and produced another photo that was roughly the same size and already trimmed. This one was of himself, wearing a black polo shirt.

Working carefully, Wade arranged the two photographs so that they lay side by side. Like a couple. Then he set a piece of plate glass over them, lifted them, and moved them over to an easel.

With painstaking care, Wade adjusted the two photos that were mounted on the easel. Seconds later, a white flash strobed as he snapped a picture of the two photographs, making a new one, one that would make it seem as if Amy Jacobs and Carl Wade had always been together.

It was nighttime and everything was quiet in the Jacob family's modest but nice suburban Seattle neighborhood. Until a car approached. Its lights suddenly went out and its engine was turned off, then the car glided to a silent stop in front of the Jacobs house.

Inside the car, Carl Wade checked the number on the house, then reached into the pocket of his frayed jacket and removed a photograph. The one he had made in his darkroom. The one that showed him and Amy together. The girl didn't know it yet, but the photograph was her future. Exactly as it was going to be.

The red numbers on Amy's digital alarm clock glowed 10:05. Amy had gone to bed only a half hour earlier but was already in a deep sleep. Across the room from her, her five-year-old sister, Sadie, snored gently. The girls were a picture of innocence about to be smashed to bits.

Very slowly, the bedroom window started to slide open—and a booted foot stepped in silently.

Amy slept on, oblivious to the movement.

She never knew exactly what it was that woke her. One moment she was sleeping soundly. The next, her eyes flew open to see a man standing over her bed. It wasn't her father. This man looked familiar, but her sleep-fogged brain couldn't remember who he was or where she'd seen him. And what was he doing in her room?

She began to scream in terror as he clamped his hand down hard over her mouth and pulled her close. He was wearing latex gloves.

"Nobody's gonna spoil us," he whispered.

Amy fought to pull his hand off her mouth, but the man was too strong. And he was dragging her from her bed. She kicked and punched him, trying to wrench her body out of his grasp. Trying to make enough noise to wake her mother down the hall.

In the bed beside her, Sadie shifted in her

sleep, barely aware of the muffled sounds of her sister's desperate struggle. Sadie's eyes opened sleepily and focused on the man in her room. Was it her father? No. Her father was on a business trip. It was another man. And his hand was over Amy's mouth.

She sat up in her bed, still half asleep. "Amy?" she asked, her voice uncertain.

But Amy didn't answer. The man was carrying her sister out the window.

"Amy!" Sadie screamed, her voice ringing with terror. And when her sister didn't answer, "Mom!"

Chapter Two

Despite the late hour, the diner in downtown Seattle was jumping. Most of the tables were already filled, and now a nearby movie had let out, so even more people were streaming in.

Lucy Householder felt herself starting to panic. It was her first day on the job, and she'd been making mistakes from the moment she started. Despite the TRAINEE badge she was wearing, everyone expected her to do a million things at once. The night had been completely nerve-wracking. She'd given one customer the wrong change, spilled gravy on a woman in a white linen suit, and completely forgot another table's order. She couldn't seem to do anything right.

Take one thing at a time, Lucy told herself, trying to stay calm. She needed this job. But she didn't feel good tonight. Maybe it was the badly fitting uniform. Or the way the restaurant was so overheated. Lucy shut her eyes for a second, then held two glass mugs under the soda machine and pushed the auto-fill button.

Mary, her supervisor, shot her an impatient look. "Hurry up with those drinks, Lucy," she said. Mary was a pretty, efficient-looking girl with dark glossy hair pulled neatly into a bun at the nape of her neck. Lucy was sure Mary hated her. "We're backing up," Mary said.

Lucy's face flushed. Her "supervisor" was nineteen years old, an embarrassing eleven years younger than Lucy's thirty.

Mary set down a tray with packets of fries on it and glanced at Lucy in exasperation. "What are you doing, Lucy?" she asked, pointing to the drinks. "Those are all regular. They ordered large."

Lucy wouldn't meet her eyes. She reached for two large cups and started to fill those instead.

Mary turned away, fed up. Then something made her turn back. She looked at Lucy again and paled. She pointed, stammering, "Wh-what happened?"

Lucy looked down, following her supervisor's horrified gaze. Her uniform was spattered with blood. Dark, red, thick blood. Hesitantly she touched her hand to her face. And felt something warm. And wet. She drew her hand down—it was covered with blood as well.

It's just a nosebleed, Lucy told herself.

She was wrong. Her eyes fluttered shut, her knees buckled, and she fell to the floor, shaking. Strangers gathered around, staring down at her.

Lucy began to speak in slurred, trancelike words: " . . . Nobody's gonna spoil us nobody's gonnaspoilusnobody'sgonnaspoilusnobody's gonna . . ."

Her watch read 10:05.

Chapter Three

It was nearly 10:30 the next morning when FBI Special Agent Fox Mulder parked his rental car in a suburban Seattle neighborhood. He saw at once that he'd just joined a wagon train of other unmarked cars and police cruisers, all gathered in front of the Jacobs house.

Mulder got out of the car and glanced around, making an instant assessment of his surroundings. The Jacobses lived in what the FBI would term a "low-threat" area: a quiet, middle-class residential neighborhood, the sort of place where violent crimes rarely occurred.

Mulder stepped under the yellow police tape that blocked off the house and crossed the neatly trimmed lawn. He took a quick look at the south side of the house, the point of entry, according to the report he'd been given. There were no broken windows, nothing obviously out of place.

Inside, the house looked like it was hosting a police convention. It was almost completely filled with cops. In the living room alone, Mulder counted three officers using cell phones, a plainclothesman dusting for prints, and another using tweezers to lift a fiber sample from the carpet.

Mulder moved toward a uniformed cop. "I'm looking for the agent in charge," he said.

"And you are . . ." the cop asked.

"Special Agent Mulder," he said, holding out his ID.

"I'll let him know you're here," the officer said, and headed toward the kitchen.

"Where are the victim's parents?" Mulder asked a second cop.

"The father was in New Jersey on business. We spoke to him last night. Should be on his way here now." The cop pointed a thumb toward the back of the house. "The mother's in the kids' bedroom."

Mulder nodded his thanks and started past the staircase to the first-floor bedroom. The door to the room was open.

He stepped in slowly, not wanting to startle Mrs. Jacobs. The room looked like a decorating magazine's idea of a typical all-American girl's bedroom. There were two twin beds with matching white headboards and matching quilts along with two dressers made of light blond wood. The dresser that probably belonged to Amy had a jewelry box, assorted lip glosses, and a ceramic piggy bank on top. A white wicker bookcase held paperbacks and picture books. Flower-print curtains covered the windows. Beneath them a window seat was covered with a collection of stuffed animals. It was a comfortable, cheerful room. Only the smudges on the window left by the fingerprint specialist gave any hint that a crime had occurred here twelve hours before.

Amy's mother, Daphne Jacobs, stood beside the window, staring out into the yard. Although she was an attractive woman, her face was lined with worry. She was not even aware of Mulder, standing in the doorway, watching her.

"Mrs. Jacobs?" he said gently. This was one of the most difficult parts of his job, talking to the family of a crime victim.

Mrs. Jacobs looked at him blankly. She'd answered too many questions for far too many strangers in the last twelve hours.

"I'm Fox Mulder. I'm with the FBI," he said. "I'm sorry about your daughter."

Mrs. Jacobs's voice shook as she said, "It's her birthday on Tuesday."

"We're going to do everything we can to find her," Mulder said, trying to reassure the woman without giving her any false hopes. What he wouldn't tell her was that many kidnap victims never made it back alive—simply because they were the ones who could positively identify their captors.

"Who could do such a thing?" Mrs. Jacobs asked him, searching for an answer to the question that had been tormenting her. "Who could take somebody who wasn't theirs?"

Mulder knew better than to answer that directly. People who attacked children or teenagers were almost always extremely sick individuals who felt a sense of power only when they preyed on the small and helpless.

"I know how you must be feeling—" he started, but stopped as the woman shook her head.

"I'm sorry," she said, speaking slowly and deliberately. "But how could you really know how I feel?"

All too easily, Mulder thought. His own family had once gone through something quite similar.

But Mrs. Jacobs didn't wait for a reply. She walked out of the room, leaving him at the scene of the crime.

Mulder took a breath and looked around. His FBI training played through his mind like a tape: A criminal either leaves something, tampers with the crime scene, or takes something away. He might bring a blanket to wrap up the victim or a cloth gag. He might leave a fiber sample, a bit of his own hair, some mud from his shoe. He might take one of the victim's personal possessions . . . something in the room had been changed by Amy's kidnapper. The question was what.

Three tiny brownish-red stains between Amy's bed and the window caught Mulder's eye. He knelt beside the marks. They were definitely bloodstains. What had Amy's captor done to her, he wondered, that would have made her bleed so little? Was she just scraped in the attack? Or had she struggled and wounded her assailant? Maybe they'd actually been lucky enough to get a sample of the kidnapper's blood.

He was still staring at the marks on the carpet when a man in a suit stepped into the doorway and confirmed his suspicions.

"It's blood," the man said. He was tall and distinguished-looking, with neatly cropped gray hair and sharp eyes. "Amy had a nosebleed," he went on. "Her little sister said it happened when the kidnapper put his hand over her mouth. We're running tests on it anyway."

Mulder stood up as the man stepped into the room and extended his hand. "Walt Eubanks, special agent in charge," he said.

"Fox Mulder. Any leads on a suspect?"

"A vague description from the sister," Eubanks answered. "Said he was wearing gloves but no mask. Clean-shaven, white male, middle-aged. Hair and Fiber pulled some promising bits, but he didn't leave any prints. Here or in the flower beds."

"What about the neighbors?" Mulder asked.

"Nobody saw anything," Eubanks replied. "No car, nothing. It's someone who knew her, that much we can figure. He knew right where he was going."

"No, I bet that he didn't know her so well," Mulder said thoughtfully. "Or else he wouldn't have been so bold. If he was a relative or friend of the family, the little sister might have recognized him."

Eubanks gave Mulder a weary look. "Either way, we're pretty much chasing our tails until something or someone turns up on this."

"What about this woman at the restaurant?" Mulder asked.

"You heard about that?" Eubanks sounded surprised.

"Yeah, that's why I came down here," Mulder answered.

"Seem's like a pretty thin lead," Eubanks said doubtfully.

"You mind if I go talk to her?" Mulder asked carefully. Anyone who worked for the government had to be aware of protocol. The Seattle bureau, of course, was expected to cooperate with agents from the FBI's Washington, D.C., headquarters. But Mulder knew that technically, this case was under Eubanks's command, and he was operating on Eubanks's turf.

"Sure," Eubanks said with a good-natured shrug. "It'll save me the time."

"Okay, thanks," Mulder said, relieved that Eubanks didn't seem to mind, and started off.

As the airplane made its descent into Seattle-Tacoma International Airport, Special Agent

Dana Scully scanned Mulder's short, almost cryptic message, and the case file she'd printed out from the FBI computer that morning just before dawn. There really wasn't much in the report. From what Scully could tell, it sounded like a standard kidnapping. Why, she wondered, had her partner taken such an urgent interest in this case?

Scully had been working with Fox Mulder for a while now. Long enough to know that he was one of the FBI's finest criminal analysts. He had a photographic memory and an almost uncanny ability to put together the pieces of an unsolved case. That was one of the reasons he'd been nicknamed "Spooky." The other reason was that Mulder's true interests were not the sort of felonies that the FBI routinely investigated. He was fascinated by the paranormal. He'd made it his specialty to investigate a group of FBI cases known as X-files, which included reports of alien encounters, psychic phenomena, genetic mutants, ghosts, spirits . . . almost anything that fell into the realm of the weird and unexplained. Sometimes Scully thought her partner could be summed up by the caption on a poster in his office that read, "I Want To Believe."

Scully, who'd trained as a physicist and a medical doctor before joining the FBI, felt no such inclinations. What she believed in was logic, empirical facts, and the scientific process. Part of that process was analyzing patterns. And Mulder's own patterns led her to believe that there had to be more to this case in Seattle than what she was reading in the report.

Mulder drove toward the University of Washington Medical Center, reviewing the facts of the case in his head. This wasn't a crime of opportunity, the kind where a victim crosses a kidnapper's path by chance and is abducted because the circumstances are convenient.

No, Amy Jacobs had been deliberately selected as a victim. Which meant that her kidnapper had probably staked out the house and gotten information on her. Certainly, he knew where her bedroom was. He was someone who had a strong emotional involvement in taking her, someone who'd planned his crime carefully. A psychotic who had a long-term fantasy of power and control. The fact that the kidnapper had been so brazen suggested that Amy was not his first victim. And that he probably had a specific place where he'd planned to take her. None of this, Mulder knew, was good news for Amy.

Chapter Four

Mulder arrived at the University Medical Center around noon. He made one stop before going in to visit Lucy Householder: the nurse's station on her floor, where he read through Lucy's chart. It told him little more than he already knew, but enough to make him believe that she had a definite connection to the Jacobs case.

He was still reading when his partner Dana Scully arrived. She hurried down the hall toward him.

"Mulder," she said.

"You miss your flight?" Mulder asked. He'd expected her to arrive earlier that morning. Scully was always prompt. He'd been surprised when she hadn't met him at the Jacobs house.

"We were delayed in D.C.," Scully explained. "I tried you on your cell phone—"

"Yeah, I forgot it," Mulder said, thinking of his own rushed departure from the capital. "I left in kind of a hurry."

"Your message said something about a kidnapping—" Scully said.

Mulder was already leading the way down a corridor. "A fifteen-year-old girl named Amy Jacobs was taken from her bedroom last night," he said. "Ten o'clock."

"Is she here?" Scully asked.

"No. They haven't found her."

"So what are we doing here?" Scully asked, puzzled.

"A thirty-year-old woman named Lucy Householder was admitted last night shortly after ten o'clock," Mulder said. "She had collapsed at work, suffering some kind of seizure and what her doctors are calling glossolalia."

"Incoherent speech," Scully said, translating the medical term.

"Technically," Mulder agreed as they reached the elevator. "But whether she knew it or not, Lucy was repeating the exact same words spoken by the kidnapper as he took Amy Jacobs from her bedroom last night. At the exact same time, twenty miles across town."

Scully's eyes met Mulder's. "That's pretty spooky," she said.

Mulder handed her the medical file he'd been looking at. "That's my name, isn't it?" he joked.

Scully hadn't been trying to make a pun, but she had to admit, it *was* funny. She scanned Lucy's medical chart, looking for a rational explanation.

"Turns out Lucy Householder knows a little something about kidnapping herself," Mulder went on. "When she was eight years old she was taken from her bedroom while her parents were asleep. She was missing for five years— until she escaped and someone found her by the side of a road. Apparently, her abductor had kept her locked in a basement cell the entire time. They never caught him."

Scully stared at Mulder. The coincidence

was uncanny. Sometimes, she realized, Mulder spooked even her.

Lucy Householder stood at the window of her hospital room, staring out on the grounds below. Her long, lank, dirty-blond hair fell in tangles around her shoulders. She could barely keep her eyes open. All night long, doctors and nurses had been waking her up, poking and prodding her. They'd shined lights in her eyes. They'd taken her pulse, temperature, and blood pressure. They'd drawn her blood. They'd done everything except let her sleep. And none of them had an explanation for what had happened to her at work last night. None of them had a clue.

She just wanted to get out of there. She was still wearing that awful blue hospital gown. She hated hospitals. They made her jumpy. Especially because they wouldn't let her smoke. She began to twist the plastic patient-ID band that circled her wrist.

She turned suddenly, like a startled animal, at the sound of the door opening.

"Lucy?" a man asked as he stepped into the room.

Lucy regarded her two visitors warily. The man was in his early thirties, wearing a suit and tie. He had an open, boyish face and hazel eyes. The woman with him was dressed in a neat business suit and an off-white wool coat. She looked like a serious, no-nonsense sort. Neither one surprised Lucy. She knew their type. She didn't know who they were or what they wanted, but they were definitely cops. And Lucy had seen enough cops to last her a lifetime.

The man held out an ID. "I'm Fox Mulder. This is Dana Scully. We're with the FBI. We'd like to ask you a few questions."

Lucy's eyes skimmed the identification. *The Feds*, she thought wearily. *What did they want?* Why couldn't everyone just leave her alone?

Then again, maybe FBI agents could be

helpful. "I'd like a cigarette," she announced in a hard voice. "They won't let me smoke in here."

"Are you feeling any better?" Scully asked. According to Lucy's medical chart, the nosebleed had stopped last night and the doctors hadn't been able to find anything else wrong with her.

"Yeah, I'm fine," Lucy said in a bored tone. "I'd just like a cigarette."

"Lucy," Mulder said. "A young girl was kidnapped last night. Have you heard anything about that?"

Lucy hesitated a moment, then looked away. "What are you asking me for?"

"Do you remember what you were saying last night when you collapsed at work?" Mulder probed.

"What?"

"You were saying, 'Nobody's gonna spoil us.'"

There was a sudden flicker in Lucy's eyes. A flash of pain, a breach in her defenses, gone almost as soon it appeared. But Scully saw it.

"Does that mean anything to you?" Scully asked.

After the slightest hesitation, Lucy shook her head. "No."

"Can you think of any reason why you might have said it?" Scully pressed, unwilling to let it go.

Lucy's brown eyes flashed with anger. "What did I just say?"

"Those were the exact words spoken by the kidnapper to the girl when he took her last night," Mulder explained.

His words seemed to drive Lucy inward again. She averted her eyes.

Mulder tried to explain further, his voice soft but determined. "So you can see that under the circumstances, it might seem strange that—"

"So what's your point?" Lucy cut him off. "All us kidnap victims gotta stick together?"

Mulder didn't feel any anger at her defiance. Mostly he felt sorry for her. Lucy Householder had the bruised, wounded look of someone who'd been hurt very badly. And for a long time.

"No," he answered in a calm voice. "We just want to find this girl, Lucy. Any way we can. If you know anything . . ."

Lucy decided to tell them the truth. She spoke quietly, her eyes on the shiny linoleum floor. "Look, what I've been through in my life I wouldn't wish on anybody. But that doesn't mean I can make it better." She hesitated. "For me, or for anyone else."

She turned back to the window. As far as she was concerned, the interview was over.

"Thanks for talking to us, Lucy," Mulder said, not wanting to push her any more. He was sure that the memories of her own kidnapping were still with her. In fact, he'd bet that she did everything possible to avoid them. It wasn't fair to ask her to go through all that pain again, he knew. And yet he realized it might be necessary in order to save Amy Jacobs.

He and Scully had started out of the room when Lucy called to them, "Hey, when can I get out of here?"

"I'm sure as soon as your doctors feel it's okay for you to go," Scully answered.

"They say it's up to you," Lucy informed them.

"We can't hold you here," Mulder said honestly. "You're free to go."

Without a word, Lucy grabbed her clothes and headed into the bathroom to change.

"I guess she's not too fond of confined spaces," Scully said.

"Yeah," Mulder agreed. He wondered what Lucy had experienced in the five years she'd been captive.

He'd have to be very careful with Lucy, push her no further than she could go at any given point. He needed her to trust him, and that would take time. He just hoped Amy Jacobs had that kind of time.

In the bathroom, Lucy stood at the sink, propping herself up against it with both arms. The water was running full force, splashing up on her, steam rising onto the mirror, clouding the image of her grief-stricken face.

Her eyes were no longer focused on the fogging mirror but on memories from her past. She was out. It was over. She was working hard, making a new life for herself. So why did it feel like it was all happening again?

Chapter Five

A light rain was falling. The sky was heavy and gray, the air chill. Thick forest edged both sides of the two-lane blacktop. It was a lonely stretch of road, several hours from Seattle, traveled mostly by logging trucks.

Carl Wade stood by the side of the road, peering into the trunk of his car, staring at the girl who lay there bound and gagged.

Things were not going the way he'd planned. But he'd never tell her that. He watched her chest rising and falling with each breath. Watched the fear in her eyes. She was terrified. But that was only because she didn't understand. And that would change. Soon she'd understand.

He turned at the sound of a horn, and his eyes narrowed with anger as an orange tow truck, its amber lights flashing, pulled up on the shoulder behind him. Wade cursed silently. First a flat and now some helpful good Samaritan. This was exactly what he *didn't* need. He gave a last glance inside the trunk, then slammed it shut.

The driver of the tow truck, a young man in green coveralls, hopped down from the cab. Longish blond hair stuck out beneath his green cap. He was young and rugged, the kind of guy who always got all the girls, the kind Wade had always hated.

"You the one who called for a tow?" the driver asked in a friendly tone.

"No, not me," Wade said quickly, hoping the guy would just leave.

The driver checked the clipboard he was carrying and moved toward Wade. "Gary Mosier?"

"No, uh, wrong guy." Wade knew he had to play it cool. He couldn't afford to arouse any suspicion. But he could feel himself growing hot with frustration. This wasn't supposed to happen. No one was supposed to see him. No one was supposed to—

"Well, since I'm out here," the driver said good-naturedly, "I might as well give you a hand."

"That's okay," Wade said, trying to keep his voice calm. Was the guy deaf? "We'll be fine."

The tow-truck driver glanced down at Wade's blown-out tire. The wheel cover was off, and the tire was completely flat. The car had already been jacked up. An X-shaped tire iron lay on the asphalt.

"Blown sidewall," the young man said sympathetically. "You're going to need a new tire."

"Yeah," Wade said. "Looks that way."

"You got a spare in the trunk?" the driver asked.

"Yeah . . ." Wade said, looking uncomfortable. The trunk. If anyone knew what he had in his trunk . . .

"Twenty bucks cash," the driver offered in a friendly voice. "My boss don't gotta know about it. I'll have you back on the road in five minutes."

"I can't pay," Wade said, hoping that would finally get rid of him. Why couldn't the guy just take a hint?

"Make it ten. Pop the trunk, take me five minutes max."

Wade couldn't stand another second of this. White-hot rage coursed through him. Without warning, he reached down and grabbed the tire iron. Holding it threateningly in his hand, he advanced on the driver.

"Leave me alone!" Wade shouted.

The driver skittered backward into the road, Wade looming over him—just as a car coming the other way passed by. The car laid on its horn and swerved.

"Hey, man!" the tow-truck driver said, angry and surprised. "What the hell's your problem?" He backed away, retreating toward his truck.

Wade was shaking with fury, completely out of control. "Leave me alone!" he shouted. "Just get outta here!"

"Hey, I'm gone," the younger man assured him. He threw open the door of the tow truck and hoisted himself into the cab. "Lunatic," he muttered as he started the truck and threw it into gear. He stepped hard on the gas and called out "Freak!" as he blazed past Wade.

Wade remained standing on the shoulder, the tire iron still raised. He lowered it only when the tow truck became an orange speck in the distance.

That stupid kid, he thought. His heart was still pounding. *Nobody's gonna spoil us. Nobody.*

Chapter Six

At 1:53 that afternoon, Mulder checked in at the FBI's Seattle regional field office. The second he stepped inside, he recognized the familiar feel of the agency pressing full throttle on a case. The office was a hive of activity. Agents were taking calls, searching through computer files, poring over maps and faxes. Most of them had worked straight through the night. Their eyes were red-rimmed, their desks strewn with coffee cups and fast-food containers. All of them were working on the Amy Jacobs case, because they knew that the first forty-eight hours after a kidnapping were the most critical. After that, Amy's chances of returning home alive would drop dramatically.

Agent-in-charge Eubanks was on the

phone as Mulder walked through the crowded room, searching for Scully.

"Mulder," Eubanks called out. He put the receiver down for a moment. "Lucy Householder. You get anywhere on that?"

"Working on it," Mulder replied, not wanting to encourage Eubanks's interest in Lucy.

Mulder still didn't understand just how Lucy was connected to Amy's disappearance. He was certain of only two things: that Lucy was a link and that she was very fragile. Mulder wanted her cooperation, and he was fairly certain he'd never get it if she was subjected to the kind of relentless cross-examination Eubanks was likely to order.

Eubanks gestured toward the phone. "I got one of my guys on the line. He says Householder has a criminal record. Prostitution, narcotics convictions. She's done some time."

"Doesn't surprise me," Mulder said. "Given her history."

Before becoming an FBI agent, Mulder

had studied psychology at Oxford University. As a psychologist, he was familiar with the aftereffects commonly suffered by kidnap victims. People who'd been held captive often developed severe emotional, physical, and psychological problems. Insomnia, loss of appetite, unpredictable tempers, and a sense of isolation were just the start of the list. The longer a victim had been held, the more severe the symptoms.

"She's also got a boyfriend who's doing time for assault and child endangerment," Eubanks went on. "Used to live with him up in the hills. She's in a halfway house now. Pretty sketchy characters."

"I don't think she's involved," Mulder said flatly.

"Closest thing I got right now to a lead," Eubanks said. "I can shift some men over to you—"

"No," Mulder said. "Let me follow up on it. Thanks."

Mulder moved off before Eubanks could argue. Briefly, he considered the information about Lucy's boyfriend. If the guy was currently doing time, then he obviously wasn't the one who had kidnapped Amy. There were, of course, such things as kidnapping rings, but Mulder couldn't see Lucy being part of anything that complicated. Kidnapping rings usually tried to make some sort of profit from the victim. And Lucy Householder worked in a diner. She'd hardly need a job like that if she was collecting ransom money. Besides, there was something about Lucy that convinced Mulder she couldn't be an accomplice in this case.

Scully hurried toward him, carrying a file. "Mulder," she said, her voice urgent. "I've got something. Something weird."

"What?" Mulder asked, curious.

"I was going over Lucy Householder's medical workup and something hit me. Lucy's blood type is O-positive."

"Yeah?"

"Forensics lifted *two* blood types off her work clothes. O-positive and B-positive. Two guesses as to what Amy Jacobs's blood type is."

41

Mulder had fully expected that Scully would turn up something no else had. She was one of the best agents he'd ever worked with. But he hadn't been expecting anything like this. It didn't make sense.

"How could it be Amy Jacobs's blood?" he asked. "Lucy was all the way across town at the time."

"I don't know, Mulder," Scully said. "But it begs the question—"

"Why? Because it matches the victim's blood type? How many people have B-positive blood, Scully—one in five? That's got to be hundreds of thousands of people in the local population alone."

"We're not talking about the local population," Scully argued. "We're talking about a woman who's tied to this case with someone else's blood on her uniform."

"Lucy is a victim, Scully," Mulder said clearly. "Just like Amy Jacobs. If she's got any connection to this case, that's the extent of it."

"Well, we'll know soon enough," Scully said.

"What are you talking about?"

"I'm running a PCR on the blood to see if there's a DNA match."

Mulder thought this over. He doubted that the B-positive blood on Lucy's uniform was Amy's, but he wasn't about to take any chances. "Do me a favor and keep that under your hat?"

"Why?" Scully asked.

"Because I don't want Lucy Householder treated like a suspect in this case until it's absolutely certain that she is one," Mulder replied. "Okay?"

He didn't give Scully a chance to answer. He walked away, more convinced than ever that Lucy was the key that would open this case.

Chapter Seven

The inside of Seattle's Bright Angel Halfway House wasn't luxurious or even cheerful. But it was quiet and clean, a decent place for people recovering from drug habits. It offered food and shelter and the company of others who understood. Bright Angel was a way to get off the streets. It was where you stayed while you got your life together.

At 7:19 that evening, a young man with long dark hair and a worried expression hurried over the threadbare carpet and up the wooden stairs. He was carrying a folded wool blanket.

He crossed the second-floor landing to a hallway and then opened one of the doors on the hall without knocking.

He closed the door behind him, his

attention on the young woman lying on the narrow bed, curled up in a ball. Although she was covered with a sheet, a blanket, and the bedspread, she was shivering violently.

"Lucy?" he said, his voice filled with concern.

Lucy. Henry had never gotten the full story on her. The only thing he really knew about Lucy Householder was that she didn't like to talk about her past. That wasn't unusual at Bright Angel. Plenty of the residents had pasts they wanted to forget, himself included. And Lucy, like most of them, didn't give her trust easily. Someone, somewhere, had hurt her badly; of that Henry was sure.

"I'm cold," Lucy said, her teeth chattering.

"I brought you another blanket." Gently, Henry put it over her. "We should call the doctor—"

"No!" She turned to face him briefly. It was long enough for him to see that her eyes were bright with fever and she was bleeding.

"Let me see your face," he said, moving toward her. She was too weak to resist him.

He turned her over, then stepped back in shock. "What did you do to yourself?"

There was a raw-looking cut in the center of Lucy's forehead and a set of deep scratches on her cheek. All of the wounds looked fresh.

Lucy's eyes were open but not focusing. She spoke in a frightened voice, "It's dark. Why is it dark?"

It wasn't dark in the room. The overhead light and the lamp on Lucy's bedside table were both lit. Henry took her in his arms, comforting her, wondering what was going on. "You hold on now," he said.

"I can't see . . ." Lucy whimpered. "I can't see."

In the blackness a long rectangle of light appeared, and the man's eyes peered down through it.

Huddled in the darkness of the basement, Amy Jacobs sat shivering. She blinked at the invading light, squinting at the eyes that were staring at her. Fish eyes. Horrible pale-blue fish eyes that stared at her, making her skin crawl.

The sliver of light slid shut and the eyes disappeared.

Amy felt relieved for about a second. And then it all came back to her. She had no idea where she was. Or how long she'd been here. All she knew was that he had driven for what felt like hours. She knew she was a very long way from home. So far that she might never get back again.

And she didn't feel good. She was freezing in this awful, damp basement, yet her nightgown was sticking to her skin and she could smell her own sweat. She was definitely running some kind of fever. She'd struggled when he'd brought her into the house, and she'd fallen against the wooden stairs, cutting open her forehead and cheek. It stung like mad. What if the cuts were infected? Would he leave her down here to die?

The questions went round and round in her mind. *Who is he? Why has he kidnapped me? Why is he keeping me here? And what is he going to do to me?*

She was so scared. She couldn't see anything in this blackness. There was no light at all.

"I can't see," she whimpered softly, knowing no one would hear her. And somehow that thought was the most frightening of all: *What if I die without ever seeing anything, or anyone, again?*

Chapter Eight

At 8:03 that evening Mulder pulled up in front of Bright Angel Halfway House and saw the red lights of a paramedic's van cutting through the night. He got out of the rental car quickly, hoping he wasn't too late.

He hurried up the outside stairs and pushed open the door. He stopped a skinny teenage girl in the hallway. "Do you know where I can find Lucy Householder's room?" he asked.

The girl pointed up the stairs. "You can't miss it," she said. "Just follow the medics."

Mulder took the stairs two at a time.

A woman paramedic was leaving the room as Mulder entered. He felt a sense of relief as he saw Lucy sitting upright on her bed, a blue blanket wrapped around her shoulders.

A second paramedic was taking a blood-pressure cuff off her upper arm.

Lucy was wearing a long, shapeless gray T-shirt. Her skin was nearly the same colorless shade, and her eyes stared dully at the floor. But she was alive. Most definitely alive.

"How's she doing?" Mulder asked the paramedic.

"Fine," the paramedic reported cheerfully. "Blood pressure's back to normal. Temperature's back up. She must've just gone down the rabbit hole for a while."

Down the rabbit hole. It was reference to Alice's journey into Wonderland, a way of saying that someone had been in an altered state. Sometimes it just meant the person had been unconscious, either passed out or dreaming, as Alice had been. But it was also slang, referring to a druggie's blackouts. Mulder wondered if Lucy had been using drugs again.

The paramedic wrapped up his kit, closed it, and prepared to leave. He turned to Lucy. "You should get something to eat soon," he told her. "Get your blood sugar back up."

Lucy nodded but didn't look up as the paramedic left the room.

Mulder stepped over to her. "What do you say, Lucy?" Mulder asked in a friendly tone. "Can I get you something for dinner?"

Lucy wasn't fooled by the FBI agent's act. Most cops came on all nice and polite at first. And then they played hardball and backed you into a corner.

Mulder met her eyes. Lucy answered his question with an unwavering, humorless stare. Two long scratches ran diagonally down the left side of her face, and she had another cut in the center of her forehead—all of them raw and red. She looked even more bruised than when he'd first seen her.

What happened to you? was what he wanted to ask. But he knew from the anger in her eyes that she wouldn't tell him.

Mulder put in a call to Scully, giving Lucy some time on her own. Then he went downstairs to the kitchen of the halfway house, a large room with bright orange walls, orange tables, and a wide stove set beneath a shelf filled with pots and pans.

Lucy sat at one of the tables, mechanically spooning clear broth from a bowl. To Mulder it was a depressing, institutional place to eat. He'd tried to convince Lucy to let him take her out to a restaurant but she'd insisted on staying here, like an animal refusing to leave its burrow. Mulder wondered if the young, long-haired man hovering behind them at the stove had anything to do with her decision. The young man seemed to be in his early twenties. He was wearing an open gray shirt over a black T-shirt and black jeans, and he was earnestly pretending to clean the gas range. Mulder was aware that Henry was, in fact, staying protectively close to Lucy.

Mulder sat down next to Lucy, not saying anything at first. It was surprisingly hot here in the kitchen, the room stifling and airless. He was glad he'd left his jacket upstairs.

"Feeling better?" Mulder asked when it

seemed Lucy had finished most of her soup.

"Better than what?" Lucy countered. She kept eating, never looking at him.

"Better than Amy Jacobs?" Mulder tried.

"Wouldn't know," Lucy said flatly.

"If anyone knows, I'd say you do."

"I got my own set of problems now, thank you."

"How'd you scratch your face?" Mulder asked.

"Must've done it in my sleep."

"Are you using again, Lucy?"

"I'm clean. Passed my test last week. Ask Henry."

Henry finished scrubbing the stove. "With flying colors," he confirmed.

Mulder believed them. "Have you ever experienced temporary blindness before?" he asked Lucy.

"I've probably experienced just about everything once or twice," Lucy replied in a barely audible voice. "And it's all been pretty temporary."

Mulder knew he needed more than her

deliberately oblique answers. "That girl's in trouble, Lucy . . ."

She met his eyes at last. "And there's not a damn thing I can do about it. You understand? *I can't help you.*"

Lucy got up, moved to the sink, emptied her bowl and rinsed it.

Mulder wouldn't give up. "I think you can, Lucy," he insisted.

"How?" she asked bleakly. "What could I possibly do?"

"Lead us to her."

"I don't know where she is." Lucy's voice became harder as she spoke, angrier. "I don't care. I'm not interested." She turned away from him.

"That's too bad, Lucy," Mulder said. "Because I think right now you're her best hope."

Lucy whirled to face him again, her blond hair flying. She stared at him, her eyes empty of any emotion. "If I'm that girl's best hope," she said, "then she's in a lot more trouble than you think."

Chapter Nine

Amy was dreaming again. This time, she woke in her own bed. Bright morning sunlight was streaming into the room. In the bed next to hers, Sadie was still asleep, the little lazybones.

Moving quietly, so as not to wake her sister, Amy got up and opened the closet door. She quickly changed into shorts, running shoes, and a T-shirt.

"Hey, sweetie." Her mother was in the kitchen starting breakfast. "Want some pancakes?"

"Don't have time," Amy replied. She downed a glass of o.j., kissed her mom, and let herself out the front door.

Amy stretched for a bit in the yard, feeling the morning sun warm her skin, feeling strong and lithe.

She began to run. She started with a rhythmic jog as she moved past the houses on her street.

"Hey, Ms. Track Athlete," called a familiar voice. She turned to see Bobby Snyder jogging behind her. He was wearing sweats and a chopped T-shirt that showed off his biceps and abs. He looked ridiculously cute, as usual. "Race you to school," he challenged her.

"You're on!" she said, laughing, and broke into a headlong sprint. She was running faster than she'd ever run. She was tearing up the pavement and she wasn't even winded. She felt as though she could run forever. She was nearly flying. No one could catch her or even get close. She was free.

Amy's eyes flew open. She didn't even have to touch the damp cinder-block wall to know that she was still a captive in the encompassing darkness of the basement. And that he was somewhere above her. Upstairs. It was only a matter of time before the slit would open, and he would watch her again. He never talked to her. He just stared at her. As if she were some exotic caged animal that he owned. She shuddered. The whole place stank of mildew and rot; she'd started to think of it as his smell.

Just moments ago she'd been running in the sunlight. It had felt so good. Racing Bobby Snyder. And before that she'd been home with Sadie and her mom . . . it had all felt so *real*. Amy shut her eyes, hoping the dream would come back, somehow miraculously take her out of this place. Of course, it didn't.

She blinked back tears. She just didn't get it. How could this—being trapped in this slimy basement with that sicko upstairs—be the thing that was actually real?

Amy let herself cry silently for a while. She missed her mother and her father and Sadie. She even missed Bobby Snyder, whom she barely knew. She'd be so glad if she ever saw any one of them again.

What did I do wrong? she asked herself. She

must have done something to wind up here, only she couldn't figure out what it was. What should she have done differently?

Please, she prayed silently. *Just let me get home safely, and I promise I'll be good. I'll be so good.*

She didn't know if anyone was listening to her prayer, but it made her feel a little better. She closed her eyes again and pictured her mother working at her desk, her father raking the lawn, Sadie making her usual mess of her side of their room. All of them eating dinner together. Bobby Snyder asking her out. Going to a concert with Bobby. Kissing him good night. Then curling up in her room with Sadie, reading her a picture book . . . finally, Amy slept again.

She woke to a clicking sound. An odd mechanical clicking sound. A thin red beam of light appeared in the blackness. And it was moving. Flashing. Getting closer to her. Seeming to float through the heavy, dark air until it was on her body.

A blinding white flash suddenly exploded in the darkness. Then the red light again. Following her. Chasing her.

Terrified, Amy got up and stumbled toward another corner of the basement. A high-pitched electronic whine sounded, grating on her nerves like a fingernail on a blackboard. From somewhere in the basement the strobing red dot appeared again. This time it found her more quickly. It was on her face in seconds—and then another white flash seared the darkness. It was coming from her left now. And the whining sound again, like an insect, only too regular, too perfect.

Amy turned away as another blinding flash erupted from the right.

Now she could see the source of the red dot, winking in the depths of the room: a small beam, like a tiny flashlight, darting around her.

Another flash and she could discern the dim outline of the man. He took a step closer. He was holding a camera. And somehow this scared her as much as if he'd been holding a weapon. It was sick. Perverse. He was hunting her, trying to pin her with his lens.

Amy sank down in a corner, cowering from the unrelenting flash. "Who . . . who are you?" she asked.

But the only response was the blinding light of the flash.

"What do you want?" Amy was pleading now. "*Why* are you doing this to me?"

He moved even closer. Amy looked up at him, knowing there was no escape. Tears began to fill her eyes.

"I want to go home . . ." she said, her voice quavering.

But there was still no response from the man with the camera. The blinding white light flashed relentlessly, the lens whirred open, and the image of Amy Jacobs, broken and crying, burned onto roll after roll of film.

Chapter Ten

The screen of the video monitor showed a grim scene recorded on black-and-white film. It had been shot quite a while ago under dim lighting, and the images were grainy. Still, Mulder could easily make out what was happening, and he watched, riveted.

The video showed a thirteen-year-old girl with straight blond hair, huddled in the corner of a room. She was lying on the floor, curled on her side in the fetal position, one hand covering her eyes. She was wearing a hospital gown and was bare-legged except for a pair of socks. She was making odd little crying sounds. To Mulder it was clear that she was terrified, her spirit broken. Like an animal that's been beaten over and over again.

Behind the girl a woman's reassuring voice said, "You don't want to talk to me? You don't want to come sit by me?"

The girl was silently obstinate. Either that or incapable of moving, Mulder thought as he watched the old tape. He was by himself in an office at the Seattle bureau. This was the second time he'd watched the tape. It both fascinated and chilled him. And it underscored the urgency of finding Amy Jacobs fast.

He turned as he heard Scully open the door to the cubicle.

"Mulder, I want to—"

"Have you seen this, Scully?" he asked.

"Is that Lucy?" Scully responded, staring at the girl in the footage.

"Yeah. Taken in 1978. The week she was found."

He turned the monitor on again. Lucy continued to resist the woman, whose hand now reached into the frame.

"How about if you just come out into the light?" the woman asked, deliberately edging the girl closer to a window.

In response Lucy made strange, alarmed grunting sounds and backed away as if the light hurt her.

"She'd been held in the dark so long, her eyes were hypersensitive to light," Mulder told his partner.

On the tape another entreaty by the woman was met by more nonverbal responses that were only vaguely understandable. The more the woman tried to comfort her, the farther Lucy retreated.

"And whoever held her captive obviously wasn't very big on conversation, either," Mulder went on. "She's thirteen years old and can barely string two words together. It took years before she was able to speak normally again. It's amazing she's gotten anywhere in life."

"By most yardsticks, she hasn't, Mulder," Scully pointed out. She wasn't trying to be harsh, but she couldn't understand Mulder's fascination with the girl. As far as Scully could tell, Mulder was giving Lucy Householder a lot more credit than she actually deserved.

"Lucy's got a criminal record, a history of drug addiction, and she's barely holding down a job in a diner," Scully reminded him. She sighed and changed the subject. "Look, I think we got a break in the case. A big one."

Mulder hit a button on the remote, muting the sound on the monitor. He rose to face Scully. "What is it?"

"School pictures were mailed out this week to everyone in Amy Jacobs's class. Everyone, *except Amy.*"

"Who was the photographer?" Mulder asked at once.

"It's an outfit called Larken Scholastic. Now, the photographer checked out, but his assistant was fired the day after the shoot. A man named Carl Wade."

"Well, what have you got on him?"

"DMV records, an old address. But he's spent a good portion of the last fifteen years institutionalized for a bipolar condition. The only thing current we have on him is this photo. It was taken by his employer, trying out a new camera." Scully handed Mulder a small school-portrait-style shot of Wade.

"You'd think the employer would have an address and phone number for him," Mulder muttered as he studied the photo of a middle-aged man with a fleshy face, light wavy hair, and protruding blue eyes. There wasn't a whole lot he could tell from the picture. But bipolar disorder, also known as manic depression, meant that Wade had a biological disease of the brain. Most people with bipolar disorder cycled between being depressed and euphoric. It was a fairly common condition, one that was treatable with drugs.

Scully, who must have been thinking along similar lines, said, "The bipolar disorder is hardly conclusive. Millions of people suffer from manic depression. Very few of them actually commit crimes because of it."

"I know," Mulder agreed. "But Wade's bipolar disorder might have actually masked a much more serious sickness."

Mulder decided to put the rest of his speculations on hold. The important thing here was that they finally had a lead—one that had to be followed up on immediately. "Has anyone shown this photograph to Amy's little sister?" he asked.

"They're doing that right now," Scully assured him.

"Good," Mulder said, his eyes returning to the photograph. Wade was staring off into space, his expression perfectly neutral. A man who might or might not be a kidnapper. And Mulder knew exactly how to find out. He stood up and took the photograph from Scully. "I want to show this to Lucy."

Chapter Eleven

Though it was daytime, the inside of Wade's log cabin was dark. The windows were small, and shades were drawn over most of them. During the day Wade kept the lights off. He preferred the darkness. For as long as he could remember, he'd felt at home in dark rooms. He never felt safe in the light.

He walked across the well-worn carpet, crossing from the kitchen area to the living room area of the house. It was all one big room. The only furniture was a battered table and a couple of chairs. Wade had never bothered with niceties like living room furniture or a telephone. He didn't need any of that. All he really needed was what he had in his basement.

x x x

Amy looked up fearfully at the sound of his footsteps above her. She'd become expert at deciphering the sounds—when he was about to open the refrigerator, when he went to bed, when he went to the bathroom, when he was going to open the narrow slot and stare down at her.

Her eyes widened in surprise as she heard the front door open and then the sound of his footsteps, heavy and hurried, on the outside stairs. This was the first time he'd left her.

Where is he going? she wondered. Did he have a job? Did he do anything that normal humans do? None of that really mattered, she decided. The only question that was important was, how long would he be gone?

Wade's house couldn't even be seen from the road. It was completely surrounded by thick woods. Years ago he'd deliberately chosen it because it was cheap. And because it was remote. No one ever came this way. Not even the mailman. Wade had a P.O. box in another town.

His blue LTD was parked on the gravel drive. He got into it and headed off, annoyed that he had to make the trip at all. He had plenty of groceries. He'd stocked up on months' worth of canned food before taking the girl, and she wasn't eating much, anyway. Of course, he'd stocked up on photo supplies, too. But she'd surprised him there. She was such a good subject that he'd used twice as much printing paper as he'd expected. And he was running low on fixer solution, too.

Driving the speed limit, he started toward Easton, the nearest town, which was a good twenty miles away. Wade didn't like going into town too often. Especially now that he had her. He knew it wasn't a good idea to leave her for long. That was how he'd lost the last one. Still, he needed the photo supplies. They were the one thing he couldn't do without.

In the basement Amy heard the sound of the man's car start, then drive off. In the sudden silence she felt herself relax a little. *There's got to be a way out,* she told herself. *There's got to be a way out of here.*

After all, she wasn't tied up. And even though she felt weak, she was sure she could still run. She stood up and slowly began to feel her way around the pitch-black basement. There was the rough wooden table. A tall, leggy metal thing . . . a tripod. The sink. And ugh!—the plastic bucket she was supposed to use as a toilet.

Something on the far side of the basement caught her attention. Was it possible? Faint daylight was arrowing through pinholes in the wall.

She stumbled across the dark space and began to feel the wall with her hands. That explained it. It wasn't a wall at all. What she felt was a thick, brittle sheet of paper . . . fastened to the wall by nails. She began to tear at the paper. Underneath it she found rough plywood boards that were nailed across . . . something. Like everything else in the basement, they smelled of mildew and rot.

Amy's heart raced with hope for the first

time since she saw the man standing above her bed. Maybe, just maybe, there was a window or a door beneath the boards. Whatever it was, no matter how long it took, she was going to find it. She braced one foot against the wall, grabbed one of the boards with both hands, and began to pull . . .

Mulder found Lucy Householder alone in the Bright Angel kitchen. She was working with a mechanical rhythm, rinsing a stack of lunch dishes and loading them into the dishwasher.

Her expression changed from blank to angry as her eyes lit on Mulder. She shut off the water and started away from him, toward the back door of the kitchen.

Mulder quickened his pace. "Lucy, wait," he called out.

"No," she said. She held both palms high, as if to push him away. "I'm done with you."

"Please . . ."

She reached the door, twisted the knob and pulled. Lucy swore under her breath. The door was stuck again, its wooden frame swollen by the damp weather. Frustrated, Lucy tugged on the doorknob. Her body froze as she felt Mulder put a gentle hand on her shoulder.

"Look . . ." he said.

"Don't touch me." She pulled away from him, a long-held fear in her eyes.

Mulder immediately took a step backward, alarmed by the undisguised terror in the young woman's voice.

"I-I don't . . . like to be touched," Lucy explained.

"I'm sorry," Mulder said at once.

Lucy studied the FBI agent with surprise. It sounded like he actually meant it. That was a first for her.

Mulder watched Lucy curiously. Her eyes were softer, not quite as terrified as they'd been a few seconds ago. Something in her had just shifted, he realized. He wondered if he was getting any closer to winning her trust. If that was even possible.

Okay, Lucy told herself, *maybe he's not as*

bad as the others. But that didn't mean she wanted to answer all his nosy questions. She turned back to the door and this time managed to pull it open.

She stood for a moment, feeling the light from outside wash over her. Quietly, she said, "I was doing okay, you know? Until this." She hesitated, as though lost in thought, then her voice hardened into weary cynicism. "It figures."

Mulder reached into one of the inner pockets of his coat. "I'd like to show you a picture," he said.

He withdrew the photograph of Carl Wade and held it out to Lucy.

Mulder felt a stab of guilt as he saw the terror take over again. Lucy's face went white, her body rigid with horror. Mulder knew without a doubt that she recognized Wade. And he'd lay money on the fact that it was Wade who haunted all her dreams.

Chapter Twelve

Amy clawed frantically at the plywood boards. They weren't loosening at all. But she wasn't giving up. She had to get out before he came back, and that could be any minute now. She wished she had a watch. She wished she knew how long he'd been gone, how long she'd been pulling at these stubborn boards.

She yanked at them again, laughing a little hysterically at her own wish for a watch. What she really needed was a crowbar or a power saw. She had a sudden image of her dad, working in the garage, making the window seat for her room. What she *really* needed was her dad.

She felt her heart quicken with hope as one of the rotting boards began to give just a little. Was she imagining it? No, it was definitely coming loose. She kept pulling at it, ignoring the fact that her hands were sore and the muscles in her arms ached.

Then she heard something that made her freeze. The sound of a car coming slowly up the gravel drive. She took a deep breath and kept pulling . . .

Carl Wade got out of his car, carrying several bags of photo supplies from Bilton's Photo. He walked toward the front door, thinking about his purchases. He'd bought the fixer solution, more developer, more film, and five thick packs of paper. That ought to keep him for a while. The price on the paper had gone up again, and it had already been expensive. But he'd shelled out the money without question. It was his one luxury. No, it was a *necessity*. After all, there were many more photographs of Amy Jacobs that he still had to take . . .

Mulder winced inwardly as Lucy cowered from him. Her back was against the kitchen door, her body shaking. This was not what he wanted. Lucy Householder had already known plenty of fear in her life. She didn't need more—especially from someone who was supposed to be protecting the public. But Mulder knew he had no choice. He couldn't undo what had happened to Lucy. And he still had a chance to save Amy Jacobs from a similar fate.

Moving slowly, he approached the trembling woman, still holding out the photograph of Wade.

"You know him, don't you?" he asked softly.

Lucy didn't answer. She bolted out the open doorway, into the bright light of day.

"Lucy . . ." he called.

But Lucy was running as though she'd never stop.

Mulder sighed and started after her.

Amy had stopped caring whether or not he heard her. One of the boards was almost loose. She pulled harder on the rotten section of plywood. A small, splintered piece came off in her hand. Daylight exploded through the hole, and she could taste sweet, fresh air. Amy nearly wept with joy. But she couldn't afford to stop now. He was in the house. She could hear his heavy tread, crossing the kitchen floor, going toward the room where he slept.

And she was close. She was so close. She kept working, tearing at the wood surrounding the hole she'd made. She nearly fell backward as a large piece came off in her hand, revealing a patch of daylight. The space was small, but it was big enough, she knew. Big enough to squeeze through . . .

Wade started toward his bedroom, then stopped. Something was wrong. There was something in the house that shouldn't be there. A noise. Was it coming from outside? No. He listened more carefully.

It was coming from the basement.

Wade dropped the bags he was holding. He got to his knees and rolled up the filthy carpet that covered the trapdoor to the cellar.

Quickly, he lifted it—just in time to see Amy's body wriggling through the broken window he'd boarded up.

Wade began to shake with fury . . .

Amy didn't know if he'd heard her, didn't care. All that mattered was getting away. She forced herself through the narrow opening and then dropped to the damp ground below.

She was out! She stumbled to her feet, her eyes scrunched shut against the dazzling brightness of full daylight. When she could open them again, she saw that she was surrounded on all sides by woods. Thick, towering evergreens, wilderness in every direction. Amy didn't stop to think about which way she should go. She just bolted for the dense forest ahead.

Running didn't feel the way it had in her dream—a joyous cruise into freedom. Her body was weak and every stride was an effort. Desperate, Amy forced herself to move faster, farther from the house, deeper into the woods. The trees were thick here, which was good because they might hide her. Bad because they made it hard to run. The forest floor was an obstacle course. She found herself jumping over huge logs that were covered with slippery moss. All around her were chest-high bushes covered with sharp thorns that snagged on her nightgown and drew blood.

Amy ran farther and farther into the woods. She had no idea of where she was. Or where *he* was. All she knew was that she had to keep running. *Away. Just get away from him.* She'd find a house, a road, a town. Someone who would help her. She pushed her way through thick branches, winced but didn't stop as more of the thorns tore at her. Trees whipped past her, surrounding her with a blur of green. *I'm getting away*, she told herself. *I'm getting away.*

Outside Bright Angel, Lucy Householder was also fleeing. Panicked, frantic, she ran with no idea of where she was going. *Away*, she thought. She ran, ran as though her life depended on it. The neighborhood around the halfway house disappeared. She was running through trees, through a dense green forest. She paused, wondering which way to go. Her heart was hammering, her breathing labored, her chest aching.

Which way? she wondered frantically. Which way should she go to escape him? She started running again. *I'm getting away*, she told herself. *I'm getting away*.

Amy paused, her breath coming in ragged gasps, and scanned the endless acres of trees around her. There was no right way, she decided. She just had to keep moving, to put as much distance between herself and him as she could.

She ran into a clearing where a trail led down the side of the mountain. She had a sharp ache in her side, and her lungs were burning, but she didn't dare slow down. She was racing toward freedom, running for her life.

Terror froze her breath as someone emerged from a stand of trees, directly in her path.

No, it couldn't be. It couldn't.

He was breathing hard, too, his pale face scarlet with anger.

No! Don't give up! she told herself.

She flew past him, raced ahead—only to feel her feet slide out from under her as she scrambled across a moss-covered stone. Her arms flailed wildly, but she couldn't keep her balance.

Amy cried out as she felt herself tumbling faster and faster down the side of a rocky bank. Seconds later, she landed hard, coming to a stop against a thick cedar log. At first, she didn't feel anything. Then the shock faded, and she clutched her arm and screamed in pain . . .

Chapter Thirteen

Mulder watched, alarmed, as seemingly for no reason, Lucy fell to the sidewalk, clutching her arm and screaming in pain.

He approached her quickly and knelt by her side.

The young woman's eyes were wild with terror.

"Let me see," he said, gently probing her arm. A sense of relief went through him as he realized nothing was broken.

"What's happening to me?" Lucy asked him in a broken voice. She began to cry, her thin frame heaving with long, shuddering sobs.

Mulder helped her to her feet, wondering what she was actually running from.

x x x

Half an hour and a cup of herbal tea later, Lucy sat on the edge of her bed, holding the photograph of Wade.

"He's probably changed a lot over the last seventeen years," Mulder said gently. "Did you even know his name?"

Lucy shook her head, then carefully laid the photograph facedown on the gray bedspread.

"His name is Carl Wade," Mulder said. "He worked as a photographer's assistant. School pictures, mostly. That's where he saw Amy Jacobs."

Lucy raised her eyes to Mulder's and said in a soft, childlike voice, "So what do you want from me?"

"I want you to tell me what you're going through," Mulder said carefully. "It may feel good to tell somebody."

Lucy regarded him closely. Maybe, she thought, just maybe he was someone she could begin to trust.

"I feel like it's happening all over again," she said, her voice unsure, a whisper.

"You can actually feel what Amy's experiencing, can't you?" Mulder asked.

Mulder felt his hopes rise as she looked at him, but then she turned from him, withdrawing. "I don't want to go through this again," she said, sounding like a lost child.

Mulder was torn. It wasn't fair to ask Lucy to suffer any more than she already had, and yet a young girl's life depended on it.

"Lucy, she needs your help," he said.

"There's nothing I can do—"

Mulder tried again, wondering how to get past her resistance. "Lucy—"

A sound outside broke his concentration—the sound of cars pulling up to the halfway house. He stood to take a quick look through the blinds. And what he saw made his stomach churn.

Two FBI sedans braked to an abrupt stop at the curb. The cars were unmarked, but Mulder would recognize them anywhere. Scully and three other agents got out of one. Eubanks and another man climbed out of the other.

Mulder turned from the window. "Wait here a second," he told Lucy.

As Mulder headed downstairs, Lucy went to the window and peered through the blinds. More cops. She knew what was coming next. They were going to ask a lot of questions she couldn't answer, and then they were going to lock her away. It *was* happening again.

She stood there shaking as the agents started up the walkway to Bright Angel.

Mulder hurried toward the front door, determined to intercept Eubanks and his agents. He was finally getting somewhere with Lucy. He didn't need this interruption now.

He met them outside at the top of the stairs. "What's going on?" he asked.

"We're here to arrest Lucy Householder," Eubanks answered, not even breaking his stride.

"Why?" Mulder demanded.

Eubank's cooperative air was gone as he answered, "I think you know why, Agent Mulder," and pushed past him.

"What the hell is happening?" Mulder asked Scully, as Eubanks and his men started up the stairway.

"Mulder, the blood on Lucy's uniform was an exact DNA match," Scully filled him in. She hesitated, not sure Mulder was getting her point. *"Lucy was covered in Amy Jacobs's blood."*

"She didn't do it, Scully," Mulder said.

"Mulder, it's incontrovertible evidence." Scully's voice betrayed her own exasperation. She knew Mulder was an exceptional agent. She'd trusted him with her life more than once. But he went too far when he asked her to ignore scientific evidence. That was something Scully simply couldn't do.

"Agent Mulder!" Eubanks shouted from upstairs.

Mulder and Scully hurried up the stairs to Lucy's room.

"Where is she?" Eubanks demanded in a harsh voice.

"She was just here," Mulder said.

"Well, she's gone now," Eubanks said,

obviously blaming him for Lucy's escape.

It was all Mulder could do to contain his frustration. Lucy never would have run if Eubanks and his men hadn't stormed the halfway house like a S.W.A.T. team. Given her history, what did they expect her to do? Stay there and willingly be imprisoned again?

Mulder didn't even look up as the other agents fanned out through the building. He sat down heavily on the bed, unable to believe that Eubanks had blown it so thoroughly. Lucy had been right on the edge of working with him, of helping him find Amy Jacobs. And now, once again, Lucy was on the run and terrified.

Chapter Fourteen

Inside the basement, lit by the sinister light of the single red bulb, Amy slumped against the damp cinder-block wall. Her arm throbbed. It didn't seem to be broken, but it was badly bruised. The cuts from the bushes still stung, and her throat was parched, nearly raw. But all of that was minor compared to the way she felt inside.

She was sick. Terrified and sick. And hopeless. She couldn't believe it. She'd been so close to escaping. How could she have been so stupid? She should have waited until he left the house again. Now he'd nailed up the basement more tightly than ever. She'd blown her one chance. Now she'd never escape.

He paced back and forth in front of her.

"Please," she begged. "I'm thirsty."

His pacing became faster. More agitated.

"You shouldn't have run," he said. He was wringing his hands, as if trying to stop himself from doing something else—like hitting her.

"I was taking care of you," he went on in a clipped, rapid voice. "I thought you understood that. Why did you run away?"

Amy felt herself trembling in shock. He was even sicker than she'd thought. He really believed this was all okay, that he was doing something *good* for her. She could feel the rage coming off him in waves, threatening to erupt at any second. He was crazy. Utterly and completely crazy. There was no telling what he'd do, how long before he'd really start to hurt her. She blinked back tears, but felt them coming anyway.

"Please, mister," she sobbed, "I need some water."

"You shouldn't have *run!*" Wade shouted.

"Please," Amy begged. "I-I'm so thirsty."

Wade stopped pacing and considered for a moment. Then he moved to the darkroom sink. He twisted the spigot, and let some water run into a filthy juice glass with yellow sunflowers on it.

He held the glass to Amy's parched lips. She drank so thirstily that she erupted into a coughing fit.

Wade withdrew the glass, watching her as a child might watch an insect in a jar. When her coughing subsided, he nodded his head as if to say, "You see, I'm taking good care of you."

Amy raised her welling eyes to him. "I want my mom," she said plaintively.

That was not what Wade wanted to hear. The girl was too stupid to be grateful to him. Well, then, he'd leave her for a while. Make her wish he'd come back. Make her want *him* instead.

He backed toward the ladder and started climbing up out of the hole.

Amy's voice trailed him. "I don't want to die here. Please. Please, mister." She was crying again, then her voice rose to a hysterical shriek. "Don't let me die!"

But the trapdoor banged shut, leaving the girl alone in the dim red light.

Chapter Fifteen

Scully sat beside Eubanks on the ride back to the Seattle FBI office. They hadn't found Lucy Householder, and the air inside the car was thick with tension. Scully could almost feel Eubanks fuming silently beside her. She knew he blamed Mulder for Lucy's escape. She half agreed with him. She didn't really believe that Lucy was the one holding Amy Jacobs captive, but she was convinced that the disturbed woman was connected to the kidnapping somehow. And without a doubt Mulder was protecting her.

"Have you ever heard of Stockholm Syndrome?" Eubanks interrupted her thoughts.

"You mean cases in which a kidnap victim comes to identify with his captors instead of his rescuers?" Scully replied. "It's a lot like the way animals raised in captivity will identify a human as their birth parent. As a result of having been totally dependent on the captor, the victim identifies with him, in some cases even comes to love him."

"Exactly," Eubanks said.

"That's what you think happened to Lucy Householder?" Scully asked.

"I think there's an awfully good chance of it," Eubanks said. "Remember, Lucy was held for five years at a very impressionable age. I think it's a possibility we have to consider."

Once again, Scully found herself agreeing with Eubanks. She wondered whether Mulder had given any thought to Stockholm Syndrome; she had no idea. Normally, she and Mulder worked together much more closely on a case. But this time he had gotten himself so caught up in Lucy Householder that Scully had barely had a chance to talk with him. *There's definitely something wrong*, Scully thought uneasily. Something wrong with this case, and something wrong with Fox Mulder.

Inside the Seattle FBI office a photocopy machine spat out sheet after sheet of a flyer showing side-by-side photos of Lucy House- holder and Carl Wade. WANTED IN CONNEC- TION WITH THE KIDNAPPING OF AMY JACOBS read the caption.

Mulder plucked one of the flyers from the pile and glared at Eubanks. Scully stood next to Eubanks, her arms crossed over her chest. Mulder wasn't sure which side Scully was on at the moment, but that wasn't his main concern.

"You'll only drive Lucy away with this," Mulder told Eubanks over the background din of phones and fax machines.

"She's already been driven away, Agent Mulder," Eubanks replied coldly. "*I'm* trying to find her."

Mulder ignored Eubanks's implied accusa- tion. Instead he focused on the important thing: that Lucy Householder couldn't pos- sibly have been part of Amy's kidnapping.

"A half dozen witnesses placed her twenty miles from the Jacobs house at the exact same time Amy was being taken," he reminded the agent in charge.

"I'm well aware of the facts—" Eubanks began.

"Trust me on this," Mulder cut in. "She wasn't working with Wade."

"How'd she get Amy's blood on her?" Eubanks asked cynically.

Mulder hesitated, wondering how far out on a limb he ought to go—and as usual, he decided to go all the way. "She may have bled it," he answered.

Eubanks was incredulous. "Lucy *bled* Amy Jacobs's blood?"

"Yes. It may explain why there was so little of it on the carpet in Amy's bedroom—"

"Agent Eubanks?" another agent interrupted, holding up a telephone receiver. "Line three."

Eubanks turned back to Mulder, his patience at an end. "I don't have time for this nonsense, Agent Mulder," he said sharply. "Maybe you've forgotten that a young girl's life is at stake here."

As Eubanks went to the phone, Mulder found Scully's eyes on him.

"I hate to say it," she said softly, "but I think you just ran out of credibility."

Mulder crumpled the flyer in his hand. He didn't have a shred of doubt about Lucy's innocence. "He's wrong, Scully."

"Mulder, you're protecting Lucy beyond the point of reason," his partner warned.

"I'm protecting her because I think she's connected with Amy Jacobs. Just not the same way everyone else thinks she is."

"Did you consider for one minute that the person she's connected to is Carl Wade?"

"Carl Wade?" Mulder echoed. "Why would she be connected to Carl Wade?"

"For the same twisted reason abused children crave their parents' love. Or hostages develop sympathy for or attraction to their captors. You know what Stockholm Syndrome is. I mean, maybe Lucy developed some kind of emotional dependency."

"After five years in a dark pit, I'm sure she developed some kind of a connection with

Wade, but not the kind you're suggesting," Mulder said heatedly.

"Well, it makes a lot more sense than the notion that she's bleeding Amy Jacobs's blood," Scully shot back.

Mulder knew he had to choose his next words carefully. No one in the Seattle office believed him. He needed Scully on his side or he was in this alone. "Listen to me, Scully," he said. "I don't know how to explain it, but I think Wade's abduction of Amy Jacobs triggered some kind of . . . physical response in Lucy. Some kind of empathic transference."

"Mulder, you—"

But he cut her off, unable to stop himself. "That's how I account for what Lucy's going through. That's how I account for the identical words that corresponded to Amy's kidnapper's, and the spontaneous wounds and blood as well. I think that Lucy is somehow—psychically and physically—manifesting whatever is happening to Amy."

"Then why did she run?" Scully persisted. "If she's innocent, what was she running from?"

"Because she's afraid," Mulder said.

Scully sighed, frustrated. Mulder was always so maddeningly sure of himself, even when his theories made no rational sense at all. This time, though, she had a good idea why he was being so irrational and so relentlessly stubborn. And she had no choice but to confront him with it.

"You don't see what you're doing, do you, Mulder? You are so close to this that you just don't see it."

"What don't I see?"

"The extreme rationalization that's going on," Scully answered. "Your personal identification with the victim—or in this case, the suspect."

Mulder stared at her, knowing exactly what she meant. "You think I'm doing this because of my sister."

Even the mention of it sent him back to the night when he was twelve and his sister Samantha was eight. He remembered a bright light outside the window and the feeling of a presence in the room. He didn't remember anything after that. Just waking to find that Samantha was gone. For good.

"You're becoming some kind of an empath yourself, Mulder," Scully went on. "You are so sympathetic with Lucy as a victim—like your sister—that you can't see her as a person who's capable of committing this crime."

"Don't you think I've thought of that?" Mulder asked. "*I have.* And not everything I do and say and think goes back to my sister. You, of all people, should realize that sometimes motivations for behavior can be more complex and mysterious than tracing it all back to one single childhood experience."

Eubanks rushed in, interrupting their argument. "Agent Mulder, Scully, we've got a man on the way in who says he's spotted Wade."

Mulder, Scully, and three of Eubanks's men followed Eubanks to a small conference room in another wing of the building. There a young man wearing a flannel shirt, jeans, and dark-green baseball cap stared at the same photograph of Carl Wade that Mulder had shown Lucy.

"Yeah, that's the guy," the young man said. He handed the photo of Wade back to Eubanks.

"I offered to fix his flat," the tow-truck driver explained. "Tried to do the guy a favor and he went wacko on me. Started freaking the minute I got out of my truck."

"What about the girl?" Mulder asked. "Was she with him?"

"I didn't see anyone else," the driver said. He thought a minute, then added, "Guess she could have been in the trunk. He was looking in the trunk when I pulled over."

That didn't bode well for Amy, Scully thought.

"Can you give us the exact location?" Eubanks asked.

"Yeah, sure," the driver answered. He walked over to a map of Washington State that was spread out on a large table.

Mulder looked on with intense interest as

the young man pointed to a spot on one of the minor state roads.

"Right in the middle of nowhere," Eubanks said, sounding disgusted.

"Which way was the car headed?" Mulder asked.

"West," the driver replied.

Mulder's finger traced the road west, then followed an intersecting road as it wound north.

"State Route 12," Mulder said. "To County 15 north, and 903 puts you . . ." Understanding flashed across Mulder's face as he found it, pointing it out to Eubanks.

"Look at this," he said, indicating a point on the map. "Right off 903."

Eubanks squinted at the map. "Easton?"

Mulder nodded. "That's right where Lucy was found seventeen years ago."

Chapter Sixteen

Easton, Washington, was a small, sleepy town on the eastern slope of the Cascades. It was actually more like a large clearing, in the midst of acres and acres of mountainous woods. The town's main street was a narrow paved road, edged with the only businesses for twenty miles—a bank, a gas station, a post office, a market, and few shops. It was rare to see more than a dozen people on the street.

On a hazy weekday afternoon, Easton's quiet was suddenly broken by the appearance of three strange sedans speeding purposefully through the town.

Through the tinted windshield of the blue LTD parked on the far edge of Main Street, Carl Wade watched the first two sedans take the corner at a pace that only police cars could get away with. He had no time to waste. There would be no chance to pick up the photo supplies he had forgotten on his last trip. He put the car in gear and pulled away from the curb, heading for a dirt road that only the locals knew about. He had to out of there—fast.

The cops were heading toward his house.

Halfway down Main Street, the last of the three sedans abruptly broke from the pack, pulling to a stop before a store with a red awning.

Mulder, who sat behind the wheel, killed the engine. Scully regarded him curiously from the passenger seat.

"It's a small town, Scully," Mulder said. "Somebody's bound to know Wade's face, know where he lives—"

Scully thought that asking about Wade was not one of her partner's better ideas. "But we already stick out like a sore thumb, Mulder," she said. "If we start canvassing

Main Street, somebody's going to pick up the phone to him."

Mulder nodded, scanning the row of stores.

"Wade's a photographer, right?" he mused.

"Yeah," Scully said, recognizing his tone. Mulder was putting pieces of the puzzle together in a way that only he could. Her eyes followed his pointing finger.

The painted sign on the small storefront read: BILTON'S PHOTO CUSTOM PROCESSING, 1 HOUR.

Mulder met Scully's look. Completely sure of himself, he said, "Then he should have an account here."

Within minutes, Mulder and Scully were out of the photo shop. They hadn't gotten an exact address on Wade, but they had the next best thing: a general description of where to find his house. And the fact that Wade had been in Bilton's. Quite recently.

Scully gave the information to Eubanks over the car phone while Mulder sped out of town.

"Mulder," Scully said when she'd hung up. "What do you think photography has do with it? With Wade, I mean."

Mulder shrugged. "I've been wondering about that, too. I doubt it's just a hobby. We don't know enough about Wade to work up a profile on him, but I'm guessing he's got a kind of stalker mentality. He's got serious problems with both power and intelligence."

Scully nodded. "He might not be able to compete with a grown woman intellectually, so he preys on young girls because they're not capable of challenging him the way a woman would. A grown woman would pose a real emotional threat to someone like Wade because he couldn't control her."

"That's another reason young girls attract him," Mulder added. "Wade doesn't have to have an actual relationship with the girls. Remember, in five years he barely said a word to Lucy. He treats them as though they were his possessions. He's like a little kid who captures a gorgeous butterfly. As long as he can hold it, as long as he's got total power over it, this beautiful creature is all his."

"Until it tries to fly away," Scully said in a worried tone. "If it's no longer his, then it no longer has value. That's why he needs to photograph them—so he can possess them, hold them indefinitely."

"Exactly," Mulder said. "He can't bear to let his possessions go because that would mean he no longer has any power. If the butterfly tries to fly away, then Carl Wade is going to crush it."

Minutes later all three FBI sedans were speeding along a narrow highway surrounded on either side by forest. Scully peered out the window, thinking this logging country reminded her of the illustrations in a book of fairy tales she'd had as a child. The forest of towering cedars and firs formed a thick green-gray canopy that let in very little light. A cloak of mist clung to trees. The woods were dense and dark, almost prehistoric.

The car phone rang. Scully picked it up, and Eubanks's crisp voice came through the receiver. "We're approaching Wade's drive now," he reported. "One quarter mile past milepost forty-one, on your right. I've already called for backup."

Mulder had to slow down when he finally reached the muddy gravel drive. It had rained here recently, and the drive was filled with watery holes and patches where there was no gravel at all, only quicksand-like mud.

Wade's drive wound in from the road nearly a mile before they saw the house. It was a large, roughly built log cabin sitting on a knoll. The house was an older one, probably built in the twenties or thirties, Mulder figured.

Following the lead of the two other cars, Mulder stopped a good distance away from the house. Silently, he and Scully drew their weapons and stepped out into the surrounding woods.

Moving with practiced precision, the agents advanced on Wade's house. The underbrush was dense and made for slow going, but Mulder found himself grateful for the forest. The trees would let them get close. They were excellent cover.

Eubanks was the first to break from the woods. He and one of his men scrabbled quietly along the outside of the house, their guns drawn. Other agents, marksmen, moved in with rifles.

A short distance from the house, Scully crouched down, covering Mulder as he moved past her.

Mulder approached a low side window that was half eclipsed by a sun-faded shade. His gun drawn, he edged around to the front of the house and climbed a steep flight of stairs to the front door. He peered through a dirt-streaked window. The inside of the house was dark, but he could make out a dusty, barren room. Except for a table, two chairs, and a refrigerator, the room was empty. Absolutely empty. Usually when a house was lived in, you could see signs of daily life: food on the kitchen counters, dishes in the sink, newspapers on the table. This place had been cleaned out. As if whoever lived here was never coming back.

Mulder straightened to get a clearer view.

No, the house wasn't quite as un-lived in as he'd thought. A rug on the floor was peeled back. A trapdoor, leading into the basement, yawned wide open.

Slowly, silently, Mulder turned the knob on the front door. There was still a possibility that Wade was around, and Mulder had no doubt that he'd be dangerous if he were taken by surprise.

The door wasn't locked. It opened easily.

Mulder stepped inside, his heart pounding. It wasn't really Wade he was afraid of finding. It was Amy Jacobs. He was hoping she was still alive, praying that they weren't about to find a body.

Mulder was aware of the other agents filing in behind him. The house was dead quiet. Mulder couldn't help wondering if Wade had known they were coming. Had someone tipped him off?

Scully knelt beside the trapdoor and

peered into the basement. "My God," she said, her voice soft with amazement. "It's a classic oubliette."

Mulder felt a chill go through him. An oubliette was a dungeon. The term came from the French verb *oublier*, to forget. Specifically, an oubliette was a place where a prisoner was not only meant to be kept, but to be permanently forgotten by the rest of the world.

"So Wade set up an underground prison to hold Amy," Eubanks said.

"No," Mulder said grimly. "I think he set this up long before Amy."

His gun raised, Mulder started down the ladder. He slowed as he reached the bottom. It was dark and dank in the basement, the air mausoleum-thick.

Mulder crouched, his gun still drawn. His eyes adjusted to the dim red light as he scanned the interior of the quiet, creepy hole.

A figure was huddled in the corner, her back to him. She was trembling, making small animal noises.

"Amy?" Mulder asked, moving to her side.

Upstairs, Scully trained her gun into the abyss below. Eubanks and the other agents had finished their search of the main floor. Now they were positioned on either side of her, their guns drawn.

"Mulder?" Scully called down.

"Yeah . . ." Mulder sounded absorbed, as if he barely heard her.

"What's happening?" Scully asked. "Did you find her?"

There was no answer for an endless moment. Then Mulder appeared in the opening, his arms wrapped protectively around a hunched, trembling figure.

Scully shined her light down and drew back in surprise. It wasn't Amy Jacobs who lifted her drawn face and squinted against the light.

It was Lucy Householder.

Chapter Seventeen

In Wade's kitchen, Eubanks was staring in disgust at a stack of 3 x 5 photographs. They were all pictures of Amy Jacobs, dressed in a white nightgown. The girl was terrified, her face tear-streaked. She was cowering against the cinder-block basement wall, helpless to hide from his camera.

Mulder, who'd found the photographs in Wade's basement, had been the first to examine them. He'd noted something Eubanks was unlikely to: that the scratches on Amy's face and forehead were identical to Lucy's.

Eubanks put down the photographs and glared at the young woman beside him. "Where are they, Lucy?" he demanded.

Lucy stood quietly, refusing to meet his eyes.

Mulder, arms crossed over his chest, watched from a distance, knowing he had to let Eubanks interrogate her. Lucy was, after all, a suspect.

"Tell us where Wade took Amy."

"I don't know," Lucy replied in a barely audible voice.

"Anything happens to that girl, Lucy, and you'll be charged as an accomplice," Eubanks warned.

Lucy stared straight ahead of her, ignoring the questions and threats. Instead her eyes focused on Mulder in a silent appeal for help.

"Were they here when you arrived?" Eubanks continued.

"No," Lucy replied, shaking her head.

"You haven't seen him, you haven't spoken with him—"

"I said, no."

Eubanks was taking the worst approach possible, Mulder thought. Lucy wasn't going to be bullied. She'd just shut down.

"Then why are you here?" Eubanks pressed.

"I don't know," Lucy said, her voice flat and disinterested.

"You just showed up here, for no reason in particular?" Eubanks asked skeptically. "*That's* what you want us to believe?"

"I've been here before," Lucy said. "A long time ago." Her voice dropped to a whisper, almost mumbling. "This is where he kept me."

Eubanks's eyes stayed on her, never softening. "So why are you here now?"

Lucy looked down, not answering. Eubanks finally nodded to one of his men. He'd had enough.

"Take her outside and place her in custody," he ordered.

Mulder stepped forward. "No, I'll take her," he said. "C'mon, Lucy."

"No—" Eubanks started, but before he could protest further Mulder was moving Lucy out of the house.

Eubanks looked at Scully, who gave him a nod of reassurance. Whether or not she agreed with all of Mulder's theories, it was clear to her that he was right about one thing. Lucy was a victim. The young woman was clearly in shock. She hadn't wanted to come here. Something deep inside her—something she probably didn't understand and definitely couldn't control—had drawn her here. And whatever that inner thing was, it was tearing her apart.

"It's all right," Scully told Eubanks.

Mulder escorted Lucy toward his car. They were down the stairs, in front of the house, when Mulder put his hand on her back. He was only trying to comfort her, but Lucy stopped abruptly and jerked away from him. "He hasn't touched her," she said. "Not yet."

Mulder stopped, his eyes searching Lucy's face. She wouldn't look up at him, and once again Mulder found himself wishing he could undo what Wade had done to her.

"H-he wants to," Lucy explained. "But he can't." She hesitated before saying, "That's why he takes the pictures."

Lucy raised her eyes to his.

"What else, Lucy?" Mulder asked, feeling

a glimmer of hope. "Tell me what else."

In her eyes he saw a flicker of anticipation, a kindling of her own remembered pain.

"If he can't have her all to himself, that's when he's dangerous. That's when he'll start hurting her."

"Lucy, you came here to help her," Mulder said, sure that he was right.

Lucy shook her head. "No."

"Why else would you come back here if not for Amy? You're sharing her pain."

"I can't—"

Mulder's manner became more and more urgent, sensing that he was finally cracking the wall of Lucy's defenses and denial.

"You're the survivor, Lucy," he said. "You're the strong one. Now Amy needs some of your strength."

"She's not going to make it," Lucy said bleakly.

Mulder wouldn't even let himself consider the possibility that Lucy was right. "Amy *has* to make it," he insisted. "You have to help her."

Lucy began to tremble and make little gasping sounds. "She's cold," she said, her eyes remote once again. "She's cold an-and wet."

Lucy was shivering violently now, as if the temperature had suddenly dropped below freezing. Then, all of a sudden, she began to cough, a deep, harsh rattling in her lungs.

"Lucy . . ." Mulder started toward her.

Lucy's knees buckled as her coughing intensified. Mulder held her up as she took a few gasping breaths, unable to get enough air into her lungs.

"Here, sit down."

Mulder helped her into the backseat of the car and wrapped a blanket around her.

"Mulder." He turned at the sound of Scully's voice. She and the other agents were leaving Wade's house; a few were running toward their cars.

Scully filled him in. "They've found Wade's car a mile north of here."

Lucy broke into another intense fit of

coughing, and Mulder suddenly understood what was happening.

"They're in the water," he said as the FBI cars peeled out in a swirl of mud and noise.

"What?" Scully was looking at him as though he'd lost his mind.

"There's a river near here," Mulder said. "I think that's where they are."

"But the river's east," Scully said, "and they found Wade's car a mile *north*."

"Well, Wade lives here. He knows these woods," Mulder argued. "He could be doubling back."

Scully stared at Lucy, who was shivering violently.

"Did she tell you that?"

"No," Mulder said honestly. "But I think it's what she's *trying* to tell us." He looked at Lucy, who finally met his eyes in silent affirmation.

As Mulder ducked back out of the car, Scully said, "Mulder, wait—"

But he was already gone, disappearing into the adjacent woods. Scully hesitated a moment, wondering if she should trust him this time. And deciding a second later that she couldn't afford not to.

She called to an agent who was moving past her with a walkie-talkie. "Stay with her," she said, indicating Lucy. "And get word to Eubanks that Wade might be heading toward the river." Then she took off after her partner.

Reluctantly, the agent assigned to stay with Lucy walked over to the car.

The suspect's skin was nearly blue with cold. He could see the goosebumps on her skin. And she was coughing. No, it was more than coughing. Lucy Householder couldn't breathe.

Chapter Eighteen

He was dragging her across a river and he was going much too fast. Amy stumbled as she struggled to keep up with him. She'd begged him to slow down, but he wouldn't listen. The current was strong and icy, so cold it made her bones ache. It felt as though her soaking-wet nightgown weighed a thousand pounds and was trying to pull her to the bottom. Her feet and legs were cut from the sharp rocks that lined the riverbed. She could see her blood swirling in the current.

They were almost halfway across when she lost her footing. Before she could even cry out, the current took her and her head went under. She started to scream and instead swallowed a lungful of water.

She felt a sharp stab of pain in her

shoulder socket as he yanked her roughly out of the water. She fought to stay upright, but doubled over coughing.

"Stop it!" he said, giving her a shake.

She couldn't help it. She kept coughing, trying to spit out river water, as the man dragged her toward the far bank. She didn't even have enough strength left to be dragged. Something inside her had broken when she went under. Something deep inside her had given up. She wasn't going to make it.

"Please stop," Amy begged. "I can't . . ."

She slipped out of his grip, collapsing onto her hands and knees in the shallow water.

The man watched her, breathing hard, hands braced against his knees. He straightened as he heard the sound of sirens. They were still far off, but they were growing closer.

He craned his head back and forth, searching for the source of the sound.

Then he turned back to Amy. "Come on," he shouted. "They're coming!"

He grabbed her wrist hard, trying to pull

her up, but the exhausted girl was dead weight.

"No . . ." she said weakly.

"They're coming!" His voice was panicked.

"I can't."

Wade looked down at Amy and realized that the girl wasn't acting. She couldn't take another step. He twisted the neck of her nightgown, holding her close, staring into her eyes. "Nobody," he said furiously. "Nobody's gonna spoil us."

Amy looked at him blankly, her mind numbed by the struggle in the icy water. The words sounded familiar. And then she remembered. They were the very first words he'd said to her. The start of all the horror.

She looked at him more closely, not quite believing what she saw in his eyes.

This time the words were different. Before, they'd meant he wouldn't let anyone get in his way. Now they meant the same thing and more. This time, to make sure no one spoiled them, he was going to kill her.

With a strength she didn't even know she had, Amy started to scream. She screamed and fought him with every ounce of energy left in her. And stopped only when he forced her head down, deep under the water.

Outside Wade's house, Agent Kreski, a young man with thinning red hair and wire-rimmed glasses, paced nervously. Why had Agent Scully left him in charge of Lucy House-holder? Did he look like a medic? He watched the young woman uneasily, then checked his watch. It had been a few minutes since her last coughing fit. Maybe she'd be okay after all.

He gazed into the woods where Mulder and Scully had disappeared, wishing he were part of the chase instead of left behind.

Kreski turned at a strange sound. The suspect was choking again. He rushed toward the car, startled by what he saw.

Lucy was gasping for air. Clear water trickled from the corners of her mouth, and she had collapsed onto the backseat. She was lying down, and her eyes were open but staring sightlessly.

Kreski leaned in over her, lifting the back of her head as her coughs became deep, suffocating gasps.

"Can you sit up?" he asked. His mind was racing. What was going on? Was she asthmatic? Having a heart attack? Neither one explained the water streaming from her mouth. "Do you hear me?" he asked, giving her a little shake.

But Lucy could not and did not answer.

The agent's eyes widened as he noticed that her clothes and hair were soaking wet, and her skin was turning even bluer with cold.

"Can you breathe?" he asked, trying to keep the fear out of his voice. He spoke slowly, making each word loud and distinct, "Are you able to breathe?"

But Lucy didn't respond.

He got on the walkie-talkie, uncertain of what it was he was dealing with but knowing it was critical. "This is Agent Kreski," he said.

"I've got what looks like an emergency medical situation. Requesting EMS, over . . ."

Mulder fought his way through the trees, looking for any opening in the dense forest, anything that would let him get to the river. He knew he wasn't far now. He could hear the current. And yet he still couldn't see water. He took a deep breath, trying not to give in to frustration and exhaustion. The woods were so thick here, it was almost impossible to move, let alone run. It seemed every step was blocked by giant ferns, fallen logs covered with moss as slippery as oil, or thorn-covered bushes that tried to impale him. And yet he couldn't slow down, couldn't let any of it stop him. Every second mattered if Amy Jacobs was going to have a chance to survive.

"Mulder!"

He turned to see Scully, a short distance away, breathing hard and pointing. "Over there—the river!" she gasped.

Mulder was the first one to break from the

trees. The water's edge was lined with rough, volcanic boulders. He scrambled over them, still trying to get a clear view of the water.

Mulder froze as he saw the scene before him. Wade stood in the middle of the river, alone, bent over at the waist, his breathing labored, as if he'd just finished some difficult task.

"Wade!" Mulder shouted, pulling his gun from his shoulder holster. "Federal officer! Hold it right there!"

Mulder watched as Wade, a good forty or fifty yards away, crouched in the water. Mulder swore silently as he saw a light-colored form in the water. He knew what it was—Amy's body, floating facedown.

Wade was desperate, Mulder could tell. He almost looked as though he were going to cry. Instead, defying the agent's order, he turned and started to push Amy under again.

Mulder pushed into the water, his gun raised. He couldn't afford to give Wade a second chance. He aimed and fired as Scully appeared behind him.

The bullet hit Wade, sending him crashing

into the water, his arms raised. He went down face first.

Mulder lowered his gun slowly. Wade's body surfaced a few seconds later, and began to float downstream.

Chapter Nineteen

Mulder holstered his weapon. With Scully close behind him, he headed across the river, fighting the current to stay upright.

Mulder reached Amy first. The girl was lying facedown in the cold, dark water, her body motionless.

Mulder's heart sank. They were too late. And yet he couldn't give up. They were too close. This couldn't have all been in vain. He pulled her out of the water and carried her to the riverbank.

Scully glanced at Wade's body as it continued to drift face first into an eddy, his blood reddening the water.

Mulder set Amy down on the shore. Her lips were blue. She had scratches on her face and hands. Her skin was drained of all color. Even the scratches were pale. Her body was as still as only a corpse could be.

He knelt on the ground, his ear close to Amy's mouth. He looked up at Scully. "She's not breathing," he said. "No pulse either."

Mulder tilted Amy's head back, then sealed his mouth over hers, desperately trying to breathe life back into her inanimate body.

Scully joined him, beginning a cycle of chest compressions.

"C'mon, Amy, breathe!" Mulder shouted, desperately. "Please breathe!"

Outside Wade's house, Lucy was still lying on the backseat of the car when Kreski saw her body jerk as she took in a sharp gulp of air.

He glanced at his watch, wondering how much longer it would be before the EMS team arrived. Beside him, Lucy took another deep, sharp breath. It was the oddest thing, Kreski thought. The way she was breathing, it was exactly the way people breathed when they were responding to CPR . . .

129

Amy wasn't responding, but Mulder wasn't willing to give up. He forced air into her lungs, then waited as Scully pressed on her chest. "One," she counted, "two, three, four, five . . ."

Mulder knew the odds got worse with every passing second, but he simply couldn't give up. Once again, he put his mouth on Amy's, and forced another breath into her.

Kreski watched with amazement as Lucy took yet another strange, struggling inhalation. What on earth was going on?

Mulder opened Amy's eyes, hoping for a flicker of response in her pupils. Beside him, Scully checked the side of Amy's neck for a pulse.

"Nothing," she said softly.

Mulder bent over Amy once more, this time pressing on her chest. There was a burning intensity in his eyes, as though he believed he might revive her by the sheer force of his own stubborn will.

But it wasn't working. There was no sign of movement. No sign of life in the young girl.

Scully stopped the CPR first, realizing the futility of their efforts.

"It's no good, Mulder," she said. "I'm sorry."

"Damn it, Amy, come on!"

"Stop! You can't help her!"

But Mulder wouldn't listen. He tried even more desperately to revive Amy Jacobs.

Scully was a medical doctor. She knew death when she saw it. And she knew that it couldn't be denied.

"Mulder, it's no use," she said gently, putting a hand on his shoulder.

He acted as though she weren't even there. Scully was torn between compassion for her partner and her own common sense. She knew Mulder was being driven by grief, but his actions weren't going to do anyone any good. It was insanity to think he could bring Amy back from the dead, and it had to end now.

"Stop it!" She put her hands on his shoulders, pulling him off the girl. "Mulder, stop!" she shouted, finally getting through.

He pushed her hands away angrily. Then he knelt beside Amy, his face anguished. Fox Mulder didn't show his emotions often, and for Scully that cool control was a far easier thing to deal with than this naked grief. She hated seeing him looking so hurt and defeated.

"We can't do anything for her," she said, her voice gentle again.

For a long moment Mulder gazed down at Amy. He brushed a strand of hair away from her face. The girl seemed so defenseless, so small. If only Eubanks had let him work with Lucy. If only they'd gotten here five minutes earlier. If only . . .

Finally, drained and sick with failure, he rose, stepped away from the body, and stared into the dark woods.

In the car, Lucy's lips were still blue but her eyes blinked and she turned her head slowly . . .

✕ ✕ ✕

Scully looked at her partner, concerned, then looked back at the lifeless form of Amy beside her . . . just in time to see the girl *move*—she was blinking and turning her head slowly.

"Mulder . . . hold on," Scully called.

Mulder turned, disbelieving, to see Amy coughing up a stream of water.

Scully knelt beside the girl, and checked her carotid artery for a pulse. Mulder stood over them anxiously, afraid to believe what he saw.

"She's breathing!" Scully said. Her hands slid under Amy's head and raised it slightly as the girl began to cough and spit up the river water in her lungs.

Scully looked at Mulder, uncomprehending. Medically, it made no sense. It was physically, scientifically impossible. She would have sworn that Amy Jacobs was dead. Clinically dead. And now—

Scully had no time to ask questions. Eubanks and several other agents were approaching fast, scrambling along the rocky riverbank.

"Have you got her?" Eubanks shouted. "Is that her?"

"We've got her," Scully replied. "We're going to need an EMS unit here right away. With some heat and oxygen."

"They're close," Eubanks assured her. "We've got them up at Wade's place right now. They're working on Lucy Householder."

The realization hit Mulder like lightning. He took off at once, fighting the dense forest growth, once again trying to race the clock and horribly afraid that he couldn't win.

Eubanks looked down as Amy Jacobs stirred and opened her eyes. "I'm cold," she said quite clearly. "I want to go home."

"Let's get her out of here," Scully said.

Gently, the FBI agents raised Amy to her feet and helped her start the long walk back. All except the one agent who waded into the river to retrieve the body of her abductor.

x x x

By the time the medics got to Lucy Householder, only a deep choking rasp came from her throat. She was fighting for air, but couldn't take it in. Her face was straining with the effort, her lips a ghastly blue.

Chapter Twenty

Mulder had no trouble finding his way back to Wade's house. The red flashing light of the ambulance cut through the forest like a lighthouse beacon.

Mulder crashed out of the woods and raced toward the house, his sides heaving, his breath coming hard and fast. He felt the strength go out of his legs as he saw a body on a stretcher. A body covered by a sheet.

Agent Kreski felt a sense of dread as he watched Mulder approach. What was he supposed to say to the agent from D.C.? What he'd seen made no sense. He didn't have the first idea how to explain it.

"I don't know what happened," he said at last. "She just started coughing, then she couldn't breathe. By the time the EMS guys got here, she was already gone."

But Mulder wasn't listening. He pushed past the EMS workers to the gurney.

Lucy's eyes were closed. She seemed peaceful. Almost as if she were sleeping.

Then as Mulder touched her, moving a strand of hair off her face . . . a thin trickle of water leaked out from between her lips.

Mulder stared at her for a long moment. Then he lowered his head, his eyes squeezed shut, his hand on her face.

Lucy had given her life for Amy. Because of him. He'd told her she was the strong one, the survivor. He'd pushed her to go beyond her own terror, to help Amy. And now Lucy Householder was dead.

His body began to shake. He was doing something he hadn't done in years. Mulder gave in to the grief and wept.

Late the next morning, Scully walked up the steps of Bright Angel. She was meeting Mulder there. To her surprise, he hadn't wanted to come to the hospital with her to see Amy.

Instead he'd said he wanted to pay a last visit to the halfway house. It worried Scully. She knew Mulder felt guilty about the woman's death; she wondered if he'd look as tormented as he had last night.

She found Mulder in Lucy's room, sitting on the end of the bed, going through a small stack of old photographs in a manila envelope. He was staring at a picture of Lucy Householder at age eight, before she'd been kidnapped. The photo showed a blond-haired little girl with a sweet, innocent smile. There was no hint at all of the horrors that waited in her future.

Mulder looked up at his partner with his usual calm expression. "How's Amy?" he asked.

Scully felt herself relax. Whatever Mulder might be feeling, he was at least acting like himself again. And she had good news for him. "Amy's exhausted, but it looks like she's going to be fine. The doctors want to keep her for a day or two just to be sure."

"How serious were her injuries?" Mulder asked.

Scully met his eyes, giving her answer a certain weight. "Wade must have left her alone. There were no injuries."

"That's impossible," Mulder said. "He must have dragged her through those woods for at least a mile, and you saw her cuts. They were even on those photographs Wade took—"

"I know, Mulder," Scully said, troubled by the medical reports. "I can't explain it. Amy didn't have a scratch on her. And nobody wants to talk about that right now. Everyone's just relieved to have her back again. To have her safe."

Mulder nodded, an unspoken acknowledgment of the strangeness of this fact passing between them.

"Did they finish with Lucy?" he asked.

"Yes. They, uh, brought in the state pathologist late last night. So I stopped by to get the autopsy report on my way."

"She drowned, didn't she?" Mulder asked.

"They found five liters of water in her lungs," Scully admitted. It was inexplicable.

Mulder nodded, smiling at the confirmation of what he had known all along. "She saved Amy's life."

"Mulder," Scully said, sitting down on the bed beside him. "Whatever there was between them—you were a part of that connection. Did you stop to think about that?

"Lucy may have died for Amy," Scully went on. "But without you, we never would have found Amy in time."

"I think she died for more than just Amy," Mulder said, getting up and going to stand by the window.

"What do you mean?"

Mulder searched Scully's eyes. Trusting her to believe him, he said, "That finally it was the only way Lucy could escape . . . the only way she could forget what happened seventeen years ago. It was the only way she could outrun Carl Wade."